Dirty

This book should be returned to any branch of the
Lancashire County Library on or before the date shown

For Isabelle, who I met at the Bath Literary
Festival – here's another book for your
collection ~ D R

For Riley, a dedicated Bertie fan ~ A M

STRIPES PUBLISHING
An imprint of Little Tiger Press
1 The Coda Centre, 189 Munster Road,
London SW6 6AW

A paperback original
First published in Great Britain in 2014

Characters created by David Roberts
Text copyright © Alan MacDonald, 2014
Illustrations copyright © David Roberts, 2014
Smashed glass image courtesy of www.Shutterstock.co

ISBN: 978-1-84715-424-8

Dirty Bertie

SMASH!

DAVID ROBERTS WRITTEN BY ALAN MACDONALD

stripes

Dirty Bertie

Contents

CHAPTER 1

Bertie and his friends were playing
football in the back garden. As usual,
Bertie was providing the commentary.
"And it's Bertie on the ball," he yelled.
"He goes past Darren – this is brilliant –
he cuts inside … he must score!"

THUMP!

Dirty Bertie

The ball whizzed over Eugene and the fence…

SMASH!

Bertie held his head.

"You nutter!" groaned Darren. "What did you do that for?"

They went to the fence and peeped through a crack. At the end of the lawn stood the Nicelys' greenhouse. One of the windows had a gaping hole.

"Yikes! Now look what you've done!" said Eugene.

"Why didn't you stop it?" moaned Bertie.

"It was a mile over the bar – I'm not Superman!" said Eugene.

"Anyway, it wasn't a goal," said Darren.

"It's still 2–1 to me."

"Never mind that!" said Bertie. "What are we going to DO? Mrs Nicely will go raving mad when she sees that window."

Eugene shook his head. "I *told* you we should have gone to the park."

Bertie didn't think his friends grasped the seriousness of the situation. It wasn't any old window they'd broken. The greenhouse was practically new and it was Mrs Nicely's pride and joy. She was always in there planting or potting or whatever people did in greenhouses.

And to make matters worse, Bertie wasn't exactly in Mrs Nicely's good

books. Only last week Whiffer had left
a smelly present on next-door's lawn.
Bertie didn't like to think what would
happen when she saw the broken
window. Her scream would be heard
halfway to Timbuktu. She would be
round in no time to see his parents.
Football in the garden would be banned,
and he'd probably be paying for the
damage for the next six years.

He glanced at the house. No one
seemed to have heard the crash. *No
one can actually prove it was me*, thought
Bertie. Then he remembered – the
football. The moment Mrs Nicely saw
it she'd *know* who was responsible. The
only other neighbour was grumpy Mr
Monk, and Bertie was pretty sure he'd
never kicked a ball in his life!

"We're dead!" groaned Bertie.

"*You're* dead you mean," said Darren.

"What's the difference?" said Bertie. "Our only hope's to get the ball back."

"Good idea," said Eugene. "Off you go then."

"ME?" said Bertie.

"*You* kicked it over!" said Eugene.

"Yes, but we were all playing," argued Bertie. "It could have been any of us."

"It wasn't, it was you," said Darren.

Bertie didn't see why *he* should be the one to risk his life. Mrs Nicely knew where he lived. If anything, it made far more sense for Darren or Eugene to go.

"I know, why don't we toss a coin?" he suggested.

"No way! I'm not going," said Darren.

"I've heard Mrs Nicely when she shouts."

"Don't look at *me*," said Eugene.

"I wanted to play in the park."

Bertie sighed. He thought friends were meant to help each other out. But it seemed that as soon as you smashed a window with a football, you were on your own.

He peeped through the fence at next-door's garden. Mr Nicely didn't come home till late, but that still left Angela and her mum. To reach the greenhouse Bertie would have to cross the lawn – and he knew for a fact that the Nicelys had a burglar alarm. What if it went off as soon as he set foot on the grass?

CHAPTER 2

While they were thinking what to do, Whiffer appeared. He trotted over to Bertie and licked his hand.

"Not now, Whiffer, I'm busy," sighed Bertie. Then an idea came to him. He was saved! "We'll send Whiffer!"

The other two looked at him blankly.

"Send him where?" said Darren.

Dirty Bertie

"Next door, dumbo! Whiffer can get the ball!"

Darren and Eugene exchanged looks. Some dogs could perform amazing tricks, but this was Whiffer they were talking about.

"You're not serious?" said Darren. "You can't even get him to lie down!"

Bertie had to admit that this was true. Last September his mum had forced him to take Whiffer to training classes. After six weeks of yelling at Whiffer to stay, sit and roll over, Bertie had given up. Whiffer was about as obedient as a Brussels sprout. All the same, Bertie only wanted him to fetch a ball – surely *any* dog could manage that?

Dirty Bertie

Bertie led Whiffer down the garden to where there was a gap in the fence.

"Ball," said Bertie. "Go on, Whiffer, fetch the ball!"

He pointed to the Nicelys' garden. Whiffer jumped up at his hand, thinking it was a game.

Darren sighed. "You're wasting your time! Just get it yourself."

"Yes, and get a move on before anyone comes," said Eugene anxiously.

"He can do it," Bertie insisted. "Watch this."

He looked around and found a stick. "Fetch, Whiffer! Fetch!" he cried, throwing it with all his might. Whiffer gave a bark and raced off after it. A moment later he was back with the stick in his mouth. He dropped it at Bertie's feet and barked excitedly.

"See, I told you!" said Bertie.

"Yeah," said Darren. "If we need any sticks we know who to ask."

"Darren's right," said Eugene. "It's a football. He can't even pick it up."

"Want to bet?" asked Bertie. He led

Dirty Bertie

Whiffer back to the fence and helped him squeeze through the hole. "Good boy, bring the ball," he whispered.

Whiffer ran off and vanished into next-door's bushes.

"It'll never work," said Darren.

"Not a hope," said Eugene.

"You wait," said Bertie. "He's smarter than you think."

There was a rustle in the bushes and a patter of feet. Whiffer came flying through the hole in the fence. He dropped something at Bertie's feet and wagged his tail.

"Fantastic," groaned Darren.

It was another stick.

CHAPTER 3

Bertie was left with no choice – he'd
have to sneak next door himself. They'd
wasted precious minutes already. At any
moment someone might come out and
then it would be too late.

"How do I look?" he asked.

"Filthy," said Eugene.

Bertie had mud smeared over his face

so he'd be less easy to spot. It always worked in spy films.

"Keep a look out," he said. "If anyone comes, give the signal."

The other two nodded.

Bertie wriggled through the gap in the fence. Once next door, he crouched in the bushes, his heart beating loudly. There was no sign of the enemy. He could see the greenhouse – but now he had to make it across the lawn.

He crawled forward on his belly, passing a statue of a small fat angel. Halfway across the lawn he froze – someone was coming! A moment later Mrs Nicely appeared with a magazine and a steaming mug of coffee. Bertie looked round in panic. He rolled over and crouched behind the statue – it was the only hiding place. With any luck Mrs Nicely would go back inside.

But instead she came down the steps and settled on a bench. Bertie rested his head against the statue's bottom. Now what? He was trapped! And if Mrs Nicely looked up from her magazine she'd spot the broken window.

Dirty Bertie

Bertie looked back at Darren and Eugene peeping through the fence.

"DO SOMETHING!" he mouthed.

Darren frowned.

"DO SOMETHING! ANYTHING!" Bertie mouthed again.

He tried to think. What would distract Mrs Nicely's attention so he could escape? An earthquake? An alien invasion? What were the chances! Wait – Whiffer! Mrs Nicely flew into a rage whenever he got into her garden.

Bertie tried to signal to his friends. He stuck out his tongue, panting like a dog. The other two stared back.

"What's he doing?" whispered Eugene.

Dirty Bertie

"No idea," said Darren. "Maybe he feels sick."

Bertie scratched his ear and pretended to wag his tail.

"Is he all right?" asked Eugene.

"If you ask me, he's gone bonkers," said Darren.

Bertie might have been stuck there forever but just then Angela appeared. "Mum! Where are the chocolate biscuits?" she called.

Mrs Nicely groaned. "Can't I have five minutes' peace and quiet? Look in the cupboard."

"I did. There aren't any!" grumbled Angela.

Mrs Nicely got to her feet with a sigh and headed for the house. The back door slammed. Bertie didn't wait a second longer. He tore through the bushes and shot back through the hole in the fence.

"Well?" said Darren. "Did you get the football?"

"You've got to be joking," panted Bertie. "I am NEVER doing that again!"

CHAPTER 4

They were dead meat, doomed, done
for. Sooner or later Mrs Nicely would
notice the broken window and find the
football.

"Doo-dee doo-dee doo… !"

A shrill voice floated over the fence.
Angela! She was back outside. Perhaps
she would be able to help. Angela was

in love with Bertie and told everyone that he was her boyfriend. Normally Bertie avoided her like a cold bath, but not today – she was their last hope. He walked over to the fence.

"Psst! Angela!" he hissed.

"Is that you, Bertie?" asked Angela.

"Of course it's me. Listen, I need your help. It's very important," said Bertie.

Angela nodded seriously. "Are we looking for dinosaur footprints?"

"Not this time," said Bertie. "You see the greenhouse?"

Angela turned and gasped. "Umm! Someone broke the window!"

"Yes… Never mind that," said Bertie. "There's a football in there and I need you to get it, okay?"

Angela frowned. "Is it your football?"

"Yes," said Bertie.

"Actually it's mine," said Darren. "But Bertie booted it over."

"Is that how you broke the window?" asked Angela, wide-eyed.

"Look, never mind about the window," said Bertie. "Just go and find the football. It's *really* important we get it back."

Angela was silent for a while, thinking. "What do *I* get?" she said at last.

"You?"

"Yes, if I get the ball for you, what do I get?"

Bertie rolled his eyes at his friends. By now they should have known that nothing with Angela was ever simple. Luckily they'd been to the sweet shop that morning.

"I'll give you a jelly snake," he said.
"It's my last one."

"Where is it?" said Angela. Bertie
poked the snake through the crack in
the fence. Angela grabbed it
and bit off the head.

"What else?" she
said, chewing.

"What do you
mean, what else?
That's my last jelly
snake!" grumbled
Bertie.

"I know, but now I've
eaten it," said Angela.

Bertie ground his teeth.
This was robbery. But if they wanted
the ball they didn't have any choice.
He held out his hand to Darren and

Eugene, and reluctantly they parted with their goodies. Angela accepted two fizzy bootlaces and a half-sucked lollipop.

"*Now* will you get the ball?" said Bertie.

"Okay!" sang Angela, dancing away from them.

A minute later they heard a ball bouncing on the lawn.

"Great," called Bertie. "Hurry up!"

THUD, THUD, THUD! The ball went on bouncing.

"Throw it over!" cried Bertie impatiently. "You promised!"

Angela shook her head. "I promised I'd get it, I didn't say I'd give it back."

She went on bouncing – she'd always wanted her own ball.

Bertie couldn't believe it. They'd been tricked. Cheated out of their sweets – and all for nothing.

"ANGELA!"

The bouncing suddenly stopped. Mrs Nicely had returned. Bertie and his friends ducked down behind the fence to avoid her.

"Angela, where did you get that ball?" she demanded.

Angela said nothing. If she admitted it wasn't hers she'd have to give it back.

Mrs Nicely marched down the lawn. "You know what I think about footballs," she scolded. "Things always get broken. If you don't—" She stopped, catching sight of the smashed window.

Dirty Bertie

"ANGELA!" she screeched.

"But it wasn't me…" said Angela.

"Don't tell lies!" snapped Mrs Nicely. "Give me that ball – and go to your room, right now!"

Dirty Bertie

Angela's lip wobbled. She dropped the ball and fled indoors, wailing all the way. "WAAAAAAH!"

Mrs Nicely picked up the muddy football. Nasty horrible thing! She hurled it over her shoulder and stormed inside.

THUD!

The ball landed over the fence, bouncing twice. Bertie blinked at it, astonished.

"Crumbs! It came back!" he said.

"And we're not in trouble," said Eugene. "She thinks Angela did it!"

Bertie picked up the football and spun it round. "Come on then, let's finish the game," he said. "Next goal's the winner!"

CHAPTER 1

Bertie had just got back from school. As usual on a Friday, Gran had dropped in for tea.

"What's this, Bertie? It was in your pocket," asked Mum.

"Oh yes," said Bertie. "It's a letter from school. I was going to give it to you."

Mum read it out.

"Goodie!" said Gran. "I love bingo! Can we go?"

Mum shook her head. "Not on Saturday, we're taking Suzy to her dance show. But you can go."

"What? By myself?" said Gran.

"Take Bertie, he might like it," suggested Mum.

"ME? Why me?" asked Bertie.

Dirty Bertie

"I'm sure other children will be there," said Mum. "It'll be fun."

"Not if it's at school," said Bertie. It was bad enough having to go all week, without being dragged there on a Saturday night! Anyway, bingo was for grannies. Why didn't school put on something *he'd* enjoy – like mud wrestling? "It'll be boring!" he moaned.

"No it won't," said Gran. "Bingo's dead exciting."

"Only if you're over a hundred," said Bertie gloomily.

"Anyone can play," said Gran. "Everyone has a bingo card and the idea's to collect all the numbers as they're called out. The first one to do it wins!"

Bertie pulled a face. It sounded as exciting as laying the table.

"Can't I just stay at home and watch TV?" he begged.

"Suit yourself," said Gran. "But I won't be sharing my prizes."

Bertie blinked. "Prizes?"

"Of course," said Gran. "You can't have bingo without prizes."

"What sort of prizes?"

Gran shrugged. "I don't know – toys, chocolates, TV sets maybe…"

"TV SETS?" yelled Bertie. They desperately needed a new super-widescreen TV. Their TV was so small you practically needed a magnifying glass to watch it!

"I wouldn't get your hopes up," said Mum. "It's only a school bingo night."

"There's free pizza as well," said Gran. "It says so in the letter."

Dirty Bertie

Free pizza? That settled it. There was
no way Bertie was going to miss a night
like that!

CHAPTER 2

They were late arriving on Saturday,
mainly because it took Gran about six
hours to get ready. The school hall was
crowded with people by the time they
got there. Tables and chairs were set
out to face a platform at the front. To
Bertie's dismay all of the seats seemed
to be taken. He spotted Darren and

Eugene but they were with their families.

"What about that table? They've got seats," said Gran, pointing.

Bertie groaned. "No way! I'm not sitting next to Know-All Nick!"

"You don't have to talk to him," said Gran. "Anyway, there's nowhere else."

Bertie trailed after her and flopped into the seat beside his old enemy. It looked like Nick had brought his gran too. She was wearing a sparkly gold dress and her hair was piled on her head like whipped cream. Bertie thought she looked as if she was having dinner with the Queen.

"Not sitting with your friends?" sneered Nick.

"No, I'm stuck with you, worst luck," sighed Bertie.

Nick held his nose. "Pooh! You could have had a bath," he sniffed.

"You could have stayed at home," answered Bertie, turning his back.

Across the table the two grannies were getting to know each other.

"So nice to meet you," said Nick's grandma. "I'm Julia."

"I'm Dotty," said Gran. "Have you played bingo before?"

"Oh, I hardly think so," sniffed Julia.

"Me and Sherry go every Wednesday," said Gran.

"That must be nice for you," said Julia snootily.

Bertie rolled his eyes. He could tell they were in for a long evening.

Dirty Bertie

Dirty Bertie

Miss Boot, their Bingo Caller for the night, sat down on the stage. Her job was to call out the numbers. In front of her was a round cage filled with numbered balls in different colours. To one side stood a table piled with prizes. Bertie ran his eye over them eagerly. There was a picnic set (boring), a toaster (boring), a hairdryer (very boring) and … Bertie almost leaped out of his seat – a silver stunt scooter!

He'd been begging his parents to buy him one since Christmas. Eugene had one, so did Royston Rich (with his name in gold letters). If he had a stunt scooter, Bertie could learn tricks – back flips, twists and double somersaults. He'd be the Stunt King of the world. But only if he won the scooter. He glanced around. What if someone else got their hands on it before him?

Nick spoke in his ear.

"See anything you want?"

"Not really," Bertie lied. "The prizes are all pretty boring."

"Yes, apart from one," smiled Nick. "I saw you drooling over the scooter."

Bertie frowned. He should have been more careful. "You'd be useless on a scooter," he said.

"Actually I've always wanted one," said Nick.

"Since when?"

"Since this evening," said Nick.

"Well, forget it, because that scooter's mine," warned Bertie.

Nick smirked. "Not if I win it first!"

"No chance," said Bertie.

"Want a bet?" said Nick. "Tonight's my lucky night."

Bertie scowled. Nick could never ride a stunt scooter in a million years. He'd probably run over his own foot. The only reason he wanted one was to spite Bertie. Well, they'd soon see about that. From what Gran had told him bingo was a piece of cake. All he had to do was collect a few numbers and the scooter would be his.

Miss Boot rose to her feet. The first game was about to start.

CHAPTER 3

"I'm sure many of you have played bingo before," said Miss Boot. "As you know, it's a simple game of chance."

"*Fat* chance in your case," muttered Nick.

"In a moment I will call out the numbers," Miss Boot went on.
"The first person to cross off every

number on their card is the winner.
They can come forward and choose one
of our marvellous prizes."

Bingo cards were handed out to
every table. Bertie studied the rows of
numbers.

"Good luck, Bertie!" whispered Nick.
"Let me know if you need any help."

Bertie stuck out his tongue.

Miss Boot turned a handle, making the
coloured balls bounce inside their cage.

CLUNK! PLOP! One of them rolled
down the chute.

"Number four – knock on the door!"
Miss Boot shouted.

Bertie searched the numbers on his
bingo card. Rats! No number four. He

glanced at Nick, who seemed more interested in sneaking a sweet from his grandma's handbag.

"Ooh, lucky for some!" Julia giggled, marking her card with a pencil.

The cage spun round and another ball shot out. "Forty-four – droopy drawers!" cried Miss Boot.

Bertie couldn't see what her pants had to do with it, but forty-four wasn't on his card.

Dirty Bertie

The game went on. Bertie's luck improved. He'd managed to cross off nine numbers on his card. Only six more to go and he would win.

Miss Boot held up the next ball. "Twenty-six – pick and mix!"

"BINGO!" someone whooped.

Bertie looked up. Nick's grandma was on her feet, waving her card in the air.

"You're kidding!" groaned Bertie.

"I don't believe it," moaned Gran.

"Tough luck, Bertie!" jeered Nick. "You snooze, you lose!"

Bertie watched Nick's grandma go forward as people started to clap.

"That's SO unfair," muttered Gran. "She doesn't even *like* bingo!"

Nick's grandma inspected the prizes.

Not the scooter, please not the scooter, Bertie thought to himself.

Julia's hand hovered for a moment – then she chose the picnic set and carried it back to her seat. Bertie breathed a sigh of relief.

Miss Boot announced that they would take a short break for drinks and pizza.

Bertie found himself in the queue behind Know-All Nick.

"Your grandma's so lucky," said Bertie, helping himself to a slice of pizza.

Nick smirked. "You think it's luck?"

"What else do you call it?" asked Bertie.

"Skill," said Nick. "I can tell you why she won."

"Why?" said Bertie.

Nick looked round then lowered his voice. "Because I have power over Miss Boot," he whispered. "It's called mind control."

Bertie rolled his eyes. "You're such a liar!"

"That's what you think," bragged Nick.

Dirty Bertie

"You won't be laughing when I win the next game."

Bertie watched his enemy bite into a big slice of pepperoni pizza. *He's making it up,* he thought. Nick could only control Miss Boot's mind if he had superpowers. And even if he did, the balls were chosen by pure chance. All the same, Nick's grandma *had* won the first game. Bertie decided he'd have to keep a close eye on that two-faced sneak.

CHAPTER 4

Miss Boot took her seat and the next round began.

RATTLE-RATTLE-PLOP! Another ball whizzed down the chute.

"Sixty-two! Tickety boo!" cried Miss Boot.

"YES!" said Bertie, crossing off the number. He glanced over at Nick, who

was taking another sweet from his grandma's bag. He didn't even seem to be paying attention.

"Eighty-five — staying alive!" boomed Miss Boot.

Result! thought Bertie — two out of two. At this rate he'd soon cross off every number. Wouldn't Nick turn green when he walked off with the scooter? Mind control — as if! For a moment there Nick had almost had him fooled!

The balls spun round and dropped down the chute. Miss Boot called out

Dirty Bertie

one number after another. Bertie was so
excited he was bouncing up and down
in his seat. Just two more numbers
and he would win! *Nine or forty-one*, he
prayed, fixing his eyes on Miss Boot.

PLOP! The next coloured ball shot
down the chute. Miss Boot held it up.

"Twenty-two – two little ducks!" she shouted.

"BINGO!" yelled a voice.

Bertie sunk his head onto the table. No! Please! Anyone but Know-All Nick!

Nick stood up and patted him on the back. "Like I said, Bertie, mind control!" he grinned.

Bertie could hardly bear to watch. Miss Boot checked the winning card and led Nick over to the table to choose his prize. Nick made a big deal of taking his time, enjoying Bertie's torture. He looked at the toaster and picked up the hairdryer. At last he chose his prize – the stunt scooter.

"It's so unfair!" groaned Bertie.

Gran shook her head. "I know!" she said. "What are the chances of them *both* winning?"

Bertie sat up. It was a good question. It was almost as if Nick *knew* which numbers would come up. But that wasn't possible … was it? Bertie noticed Nick had left something on his chair – his grandma's handbag. She had seen it too and tried to grab it. But Bertie got there first.

Dirty Bertie

"Hey, give that back!" she cried.

Wait a minute, what was this? Bertie found sheets of sticky-backed numbers hidden among the sweets! He leaped to his feet.

"HE CHEATED!" he yelled.

"BERTIE!" snapped Miss Boot. "SIT DOWN!"

"But he did, Miss!" said Bertie. "He's been sticking numbers on his card."

"I haven't!" whined Nick, turning pink.

Nick's grandma stood up.

"Really! Some people are such bad losers."

"If you don't believe me, look in the bag!" said Bertie, holding it up.

Miss Boot was losing patience. "Let me see that," she said.

Bertie went over to the stage and gave her the bag. Miss Boot looked at the sheets of sticky numbers, then at Nick's winning card. On a closer look, she found many of the numbers could be peeled off. She screwed up the piece of paper.

"NICHOLAS!" she thundered.

Nick let out a wail. "It wasn't my fault!"

"Then whose fault was it?" asked Miss Boot.

"My grandma's," bleated Nick. "It was her idea!"

People gasped and turned their heads.

Dirty Bertie

"Don't tell lies!" said Julia.

"I'm not!" squawked Nick. "You said that no one would find out."

"THAT'S ENOUGH!" barked Miss Boot. "You should both be ashamed of yourselves! Give back your prizes right now."

Nick and his grandma did as they were told. As they left the stage they found rows of angry faces staring at them.

"BOO! CHEATS!" cried someone. Others joined in.

Nick and his grandma didn't wait to hear more. They grabbed their things and fled from the hall, banging the door behind them.

Miss Boot shook her head. "Well, Bertie," she said. "For once I must thank you for interrupting."

"That's okay," said Bertie. "But what about their prizes?"

Miss Boot thought for a moment. She could return them to the table, but there was only half an hour left and they'd have prizes left over. It seemed a terrible waste. "I guess *someone* should have them," she said. "I don't suppose you like scooters?"

"LIKE THEM?" gasped Bertie.

He could hardly believe his luck – and to think he almost hadn't come! He couldn't wait to zoom into school on his new stunt scooter on Monday morning. It turned out Gran had been right all along – bingo was the greatest game ever!

Dirty Bertie

CHAPTER 1

Bertie watched the golf ball roll across the lawn and into the small black cup.

WHIRR-CLICK-PLOCK!

It spat it out.

"Wow!" cried Bertie. "Can I have a go?"

Dad shook his head. "Maybe another time," he said. In Bertie's hands a golf club was a dangerous weapon.

"Please," begged Bertie. "Just one little go!"

Dad sighed. "All right, but for goodness' sake take it easy."

Bertie gripped the club and took careful aim.

"Gently," warned Dad.

Bertie swung the golf club.

THWUCK!

The ball flew like a missile and cannoned off the garden wall.

"ARGH!" Dad ducked as it zoomed past his head and buried itself in the hedge.

"HA, HA! Good shot, Bertie!" Bertie looked round to see Royston Rich getting out of his dad's sports car. Royston got on Bertie's nerves. His head

Dirty Bertie

was so big you'd think his dad would need a larger car.

"What do *you* want?" asked Bertie.

"Oh, we were just passing by," said Royston. "Actually we've been playing at Dad's golf club!"

Mr Rich put a hand on his son's shoulder. "I'm a member at Pudsley Hills," he said. "On the committee, in fact."

Dad rolled his eyes. "You don't say."

"Dad's *awesome* at golf," bragged Royston. "He's won tons of trophies."

Mr Rich chuckled. "I am pretty good, though I say so myself." He turned to Dad. "I didn't know you played, old man."

"Oh yes," said Dad. "I'm not bad – though I say so myself."

"Really?" Mr Rich smiled, smoothing his moustache. "Well, we should have a game sometime."

"Anytime you like," said Dad.

"Super. Next Sunday then?"

"You're on."

Bertie couldn't believe his ears. A golf match against Mr Rich – surely that was asking for trouble? Still, he didn't want to miss all the fun.

"Can I come?" he begged.

"Why not?" said Mr Rich. "The boys

Dirty Bertie

can act as our caddies."

"Fine by me," said Dad.

"Me too," said Bertie, wondering what a caddy could be.

Mr Rich strolled back to his car.
"By the way, a little tip," he said to Dad.
"Don't lift your head when you play the ball."

"See you Bertie! You are *so* going to lose," sneered Royston, sticking out his tongue.

"Get lost, goofy!" said Bertie.

Mr Rich drove off with a screech of tyres.

Dirty Bertie

Bertie frowned at his dad. "I thought you hated him?" he said.

"Maurice Rich? Can't stand the man," said Dad.

"So why play golf with him?"

"To beat him, of course," said Dad. "It's time I taught that snooty show-off a lesson."

CHAPTER 2

Over supper Bertie mentioned who they'd run into that morning.

"Maurice Rich?" groaned Mum. "What did he want?"

"Nothing," said Dad.

"He wants to play Dad at golf," said Bertie.

Suzy stopped eating. Mum narrowed

her eyes.

"You're not serious?" she said.

Dad shrugged. "It's only a game."

"Oh yes!" scoffed Suzy. "That's what you said last time!"

Bertie hadn't forgotten last time. On Sports Day both dads had joined in the Parent-Child race. It had ended in an ugly brawl.

"He challenged me," said Dad. "You know what a pompous twerp he is!"

"So ignore him," said Mum. "Honestly, you're worse than a pair of kids."

"I could hardly say no. He saw me practising," argued Dad.

"For the first time in ages," said Mum. "Your clubs have probably gone rusty."

Bertie wiped his nose. "I'm good at golf," he said.

"You've never played," said Suzy.

"I have! On holiday, remember?"

Suzy rolled her eyes. "That was crazy golf, dumbo."

"It's still golf," said Bertie. "And actually it's a lot harder 'cos there's castles and stuff in the way."

Dad shook his head. "This is *real* golf, Bertie, on a proper golf course. And if you're my caddy, you'll have to behave."

Suzy giggled. "You're taking Bertie?"

"I'd be more use than you," said Bertie. "Anyway, what *is* a caddy?"

"It's a sort of helper," explained Dad. "You carry my golf bag and hand me a club when I need one."

Bertie frowned. "Can't I do potting?"

"It's called putting," sighed Dad. "And no, you can't. Your job is to do what I tell you and not get in the way."

Bertie pushed some peas round his plate. What was the point of going if he wasn't allowed to *do* anything? He wanted to beat the Riches just as much as Dad – after all, he'd be the one to suffer if they lost. Royston would brag about it for months.

CHAPTER 3

Bertie stared out of the window as they
pulled into the car park. Royston and
his dad were waiting by the clubhouse,
wearing matching outfits – red jumpers,
yellow trousers and white golf caps.
Bertie thought they looked like two
giant sticks of rock.

Mr Rich's golf bag was almost as big

as him and stuffed with shiny new clubs.
Beside it, Dad's bag looked like it came
from a charity shop.

"Morning!" said Mr Rich. "How about
a little bet to make this interesting?
Twenty pounds?"

"Make it thirty," said Dad.

Mr Rich chuckled. "Suits me, if you
want to lose your money."

Thirty pounds? Bertie's mouth hung
open. That was practically a year's
pocket money! He hoped Dad knew
what he was doing.

Mr Rich put his bag in the back of a
golf buggy and climbed in beside Royston.
"See you at the first hole!" he called.

Dad nodded. "Where'd you get the
buggy?"

"Oh, didn't I say, old man? We took

the last one," grinned Mr Rich. "Never mind, I'm sure you'll enjoy the walk!" He threw them a wave and drove off.

"It's not fair!" grumbled Bertie. "Why do *they* get a buggy and not us?"

"It's healthier to walk," snapped Dad. "Bring the trolley."

Bertie dragged the trolley behind him. It had one squeaky wheel. He kept tipping it too far and spilling golf clubs everywhere.

Dirty Bertie

Royston and Mr Rich were waiting for them at the first hole. Bertie stared.

"Where's the golf course?" he said.

"This is it," said Dad.

"But it's just grass and trees! I can't even see the hole!" moaned Bertie.

Dad pointed to a tiny red flag in the distance.

"That's *miles* away!" cried Bertie. "It'll take forever!"

Mr Rich cleared his throat. "Are we playing or not?" he said.

"Sorry," said Dad. "Go ahead."

Mr Rich stood over his ball. He swung back his club.

PLINK!

The ball flew straight down the middle of the fairway.

Dad was next. He placed his ball,

stood over it and waggled the club.
Then he swished the air a few times.

"Aren't you meant to hit it?" asked
Bertie.

Dad glared. "I'm *going to* if you'll
shut up."

PLUNK!

The ball swerved left and vanished into a thick clump of trees.

"Oh, bad luck, old man!" smirked Mr Rich. Bertie shot his dad a look of disgust. The least he could do was hit the ball straight.

Royston climbed into the golf buggy beside his dad.

"See you up at the green — if you ever get there!" he sniggered.

Dirty Bertie

By the time they reached the green, Bertie's legs were aching. The Riches were waiting for them.

Mr Rich putted his ball and watched it go in.

"We win the hole!" whooped Royston.

Dad filled in the score-card.

"Come on," he said to Bertie. "And stop dropping all the clubs."

"It's not *my* fault, it's this stupid trolley," grumbled Bertie. "If we had a buggy I wouldn't have to drag it everywhere."

CHAPTER 4

The game went on for hour after hour. By the time they reached the twelfth hole, Bertie felt like they'd been playing for days.

Royston climbed out of his buggy. "You're lucky we're only four up!" he boasted.

"Up where?" asked Bertie.

"Four holes ahead, stupid," said
Royston. "And there's only six holes left
to play."

Six holes! Bertie didn't think he could
bear it. He had walked about a hundred
miles. He'd hunted in woods, poked
in bushes and slipped over in a muddy
stream. The Riches meanwhile had sailed
round the course in their golf buggy.
Royston was now at the wheel and he
zoomed off as if he was driving a Ferrari.

Mr Rich placed his ball. "Winner goes
first, so that's me again," he said.

PLINK!

The ball rose into the air – another
perfect drive down the middle.

PLUNK!

Dirty Bertie

Dad's ball skidded left and vanished into the long grass. He groaned.

"Oh dear! Looks like it's just not your day," chuckled Mr Rich.

Dad stomped off to look for his ball.

Let's face it, we're going to lose, thought Bertie. CRASH! The trolley tipped over for the hundredth time, dumping the clubs on the grass. Bertie sighed and stood it up. *Wait a minute, what was this in the zip pocket?* Loads of golf balls! Why hadn't Dad mentioned this before? They could have saved so much time!

Bertie took one of the balls and dropped it on a patch of grass.

Dirty Bertie

"Dad! Over here!" he yelled.

Dad came hurrying back.

"Is that my ball?" he frowned.

"Of course. I just found it," said Bertie.

Dad scratched his head. 'That's odd, I thought it went over there. Still, I'm not complaining."

He hit a shot, which bounced three times and rolled on to the green.

Maurice Rich looked like he might die of shock. Dad putted his ball and went on to win the hole.

At the next hole Mr Rich seemed a little on edge. He gripped his club and drew it back.

"Is that a lake?" asked Bertie, pointing to the right.

Dirty Bertie

Mr Rich lowered his club. "I was just about to play," he snapped.

"Oh sorry, go on," said Bertie.

Mr Rich swung his club back again…

"Only I was just wondering, do they have lakes in golf?" asked Bertie.

"YES, IT'S A LAKE!" said Mr Rich through gritted teeth.

"What happens if your ball goes in?" asked Bertie.

"You take an extra shot and have to play again," snarled Mr Rich. "Now if you will please BE QUIET…"

Dirty Bertie

Mr Rich swung. The ball sliced to the right and landed in the lake with a plop.

Dad grinned. "Bad luck, old man!" he said.

Bertie decided that golf only made people bad-tempered. It certainly had that effect on Mr Rich. One of his shots hit a tree. He covered himself in sand trying to hit his ball out of a bunker. When he missed a putt he yelled at Royston for breathing too loudly. The next three holes all went to Bertie's dad.

When they reached the final hole the scores were level. But Mr Rich hadn't finished. He hit a perfect shot, which came to rest ten paces from the flag. Dad's shot landed a little short of the green.

Royston gave Bertie a look of triumph. One good putt and the game was theirs. Royston zoomed past and parked his golf buggy on the slope above the green.

Mr Rich stood over his ball.

"This is to win the match then," he said smugly.

Bertie wasn't watching. "Mr Rich!" he said.

"Not now!" snapped Mr Rich.

"But I think you…"

"WILL YOU SHUT UP!" growled Mr Rich.

He drew his club slowly back. PLOCK!

Dirty Bertie

The ball rolled straight towards the hole. It might have got there but for one thing – Royston had left the brake off the golf buggy. It was bumping down the slope on to the green. It picked up speed, heading straight for Mr Rich's ball.

"NO! STOP IT!" screeched Mr Rich. "STOP…"

Dirty Bertie

CRUNCH!

The ball was squashed under the front wheel. To play it Mr Rich would have needed a shovel.

"ROYSTON, YOU IDIOT!" he roared, his face purple.

Dirty Bertie

Twenty minutes later Bertie and Dad were enjoying the All-Day Breakfast at the golf-club restaurant. Mr Rich's thirty pound bet was paying the bill.

"I still can't believe I won," said Dad.

"Only because you had a brilliant caddy," said Bertie.

"True," said Dad. "If you hadn't found my lost ball, I'd have been in trouble."

"Yes, lucky I looked in your bag," said Bertie.

Dad put down his fork. "My bag? You mean that *wasn't* my ball?"

"It was one of them," said Bertie. "I found it in the pocket of your bag."

"But it wasn't the ball I lost?"

"Oh no," said Bertie. "I gave up

looking for that."

Dad gasped. "But you can't just swap balls!" he said. "You're meant to take an extra shot. IT'S CHEATING!"

"Is it?" said Bertie.

"Of course it is!"

Bertie shrugged. "Oh well, it's a stupid game. Are you leaving that sausage?"